Written by Tim Collins

Illustrations and cover design by Joëlle Dreidemy

Thanks to Collette Collins, Justine Smith,
Philippa Wingate and Bryony Jones

First published in Great Britain in 2014 by Buster Books,
an imprint of Michael O'Mara Books Limited,
9 Lion Yard, Tremadoc Road, London SW4 7NQ

W www.busterbooks.co.uk

f Buster Children's Books

y @BusterBooks

www.cosmiccolin.co.uk

A CIP catalogue record for this book is available from the British Library.

ISBN: 978-1-78055-171-5

10 9 8 7 6 5 4 3 2

Printed and bound in March 2014 by CPI Group (UK) Ltd, 108 Beddington
Lane, Croydon, CR0 4YY, United Kingdom.

Papers used by Michael O'Mara Books are natural, recyclable products
made from wood grown in sustainable forests. The manufacturing processes
conform to the environmental regulations of the country of origin.

COSMIC COLIN

COLIN

Stinky Space Race

BUSTER

CHAPTER ONE

There is a bin
at the back of
our school.

This is my friend Harry jumping into it.

And there I am, following him right in.

You might think we're a couple of weirdos.

You might even think we're so poor we have to root around in a bin for our lunch.

You can think what you like. The truth is,
we have very important business in that
bin and I can't tell you about it.

Alright then, if you must know ...

That bin can take us

ANYWHERE

IN TIME AND SPACE.

Look at the CCTV footage if you don't
believe me.

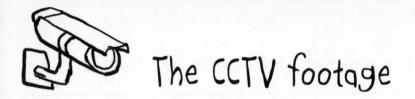

The CCTV footage

First the bin's there.

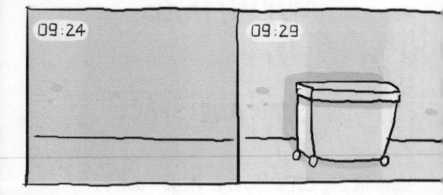

Then it's not there.   Then it's there again.

Then we emerge carrying a genuine top-of-the-range
Sonic Blasterizer.

Where do you think we got a genuine Sonic Blasterizer?

From OUTER SPACE, of course.

Strange things happen every time we get in that bin.

Like that time we turned EVERYONE in the world into our teacher, Mr Watkins.

CHAPTER TWO

Picture your teacher for a minute. Now imagine if everyone in the world looked and sounded exactly like them. <u>HORRIBLE,</u> isn't it?

Maybe it isn't horrible for you. For all I know, you might like your teacher. If you do, you're very lucky. Because my teacher, Mr Watkins, is THE MOST BORING PERSON IN THE WORLD.

No, forget that. He's the most boring THING in the world. Even traffic jams and instruction manuals are more interesting than him.

Hair (boring)

Head (boring)

Moustache (boring)

Body (boring)

Shoes (boring)

The most boring thing of all about
Mr Watkins is the way he repeats the
same things over and over again.

I told you he repeats himself.

If we don't want to fall asleep when
Mr Watkins is speaking, we play one of
these brilliant games I invented ...

GAME ONE: PAPER THROW

1. Screw up paper.

2. Throw it at Mr Watkins' shiny head.

3. If it hits, say, 'Sorry, I was aiming for the bin'.

SCORING:

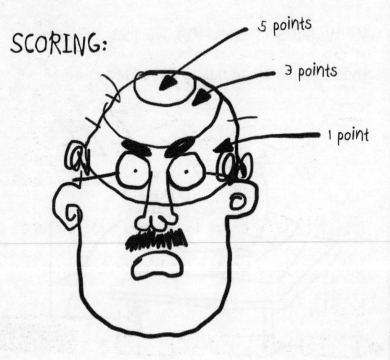

5 points

3 points

1 point

GAME TWO: SPEED DRAW

1. Wait for Mr Watkins to leave the classroom.

2. Draw rude pictures of him on the whiteboard.

SHINY HEAD

I AM A LOSER

smelly breath

SCORING: 1 point for every rude picture you can draw before Mr Watkins comes back in.

GAME THREE: WATCH SHINE

1. Place your arm in the sun and catch the reflection on your watch.

2. Move your wrist until the reflection shows on Mr Watkins' face.

3. Pretend it was an accident when he gets angry.

SCORING:
3 points for the top of the head

5 points for the eyes

1 point for anywhere else on the face

CHAPTER THREE

I was playing **WATCH SHINE** the day
I first met Harry.

Mr Watkins broke off the lesson to grab
my watch.

RIGHT!
I'm confiscating that.

He plonked it in the drawer of his desk.

I hate that drawer. Mr Watkins keeps his moustache trimmer in there, so everything comes out covered in disgusting hairs.

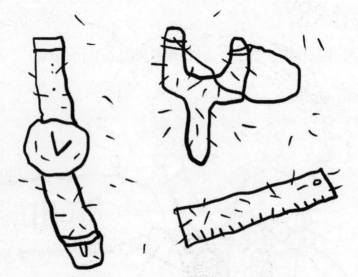

I had to wait behind after the lesson to collect my watch.

Harry was there, too.

Harry had joined our school a few days earlier. I thought there was something strange about him as soon as I saw him.

HARRY

Hair (neat)

Shirt (clean)

Tie (straight)

School blazer (new)

He looked more like someone pretending to be a school pupil than an actual school pupil.

NORMAL PUPIL (ME)

Hair (wild)

Tie (wonky)

Shirt (dirty)

School blazer (left at home)

I spoke to Harry while I waited to collect my watch:

Did you get something confiscated too?

Yeah. My space comm ... I mean, my phone.

Just to warn you, it will be covered in moustache hairs.

EWWW!

When the other pupils had all gone,
Mr Watkins gave us a boring lecture.

As you can see, I wasn't listening. But it
was probably something about how talking
to us was like talking to a brick wall.

Mr Watkins handed my watch back and I wiped the hairs off.

I peered over at Harry's phone. It didn't look like any phone I'd seen before. It had red lights on top, and the word 'DISTRESS' was flashing on the screen.

It's ... er ... my mum. She wants me to buy cheese. It distresses her if she doesn't have any. She loves cheese.

Oh, okay. I understand.

I didn't understand really. That's why I spied on Harry that lunch time.

CHAPTER FOUR

When Harry thought no one was looking, he went around to the back of the school. I peered around a wall and watched as he approached the school bins.

The bins behind the school are strictly **OUT OF BOUNDS.**

Mr Watkins goes mad if he spots anyone going near them.

Harry stopped in front of one of the bins and pressed a button on his phone.

The lid of the bin flipped open. Harry glanced one way, then the other, then jumped in.

I winced as I thought about the smelly scraps of food he must have landed in.

I was still thinking about this when the bin vanished.

I rubbed my eyes and looked again. The bin was still gone.

I sneaked over to where it had been. I knew Mr Watkins might rush over and yell at me, but I had to work out what had happened.

Then the bin appeared again, right in front of my eyes. I had to dive out of the way so it didn't squash me.

The lid opened and Harry jumped out. His head was covered in green gloop. At first I thought it was school dinner slops, but then I saw it was glowing slightly.

As Harry scooped some of the gunge out of his ear with his finger, he looked up at me.

I didn't really want my brain to leak out of my ears. It would be very annoying having to carry it around everywhere.

But I was SO curious I decided to risk it.

Try me.

Alright then.

I'm an alien from a planet in the Centauri Galaxy and I travel through space and time in that bin. My phone is really a space communicator. I just answered a DISTRESS call on it and saved an old friend from an alien attack, which is why I'm covered in slime.

Oh, and my mum doesn't really like cheese.

My brain didn't leak of out my ears. But I was rather confused.

Harry pressed a button on his communicator and the lid of the bin flipped open.

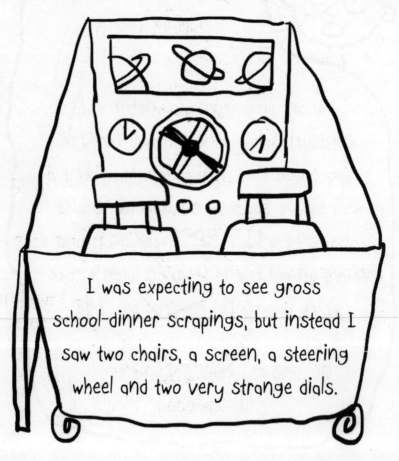

I was expecting to see gross school-dinner scrapings, but instead I saw two chairs, a screen, a steering wheel and two very strange dials.

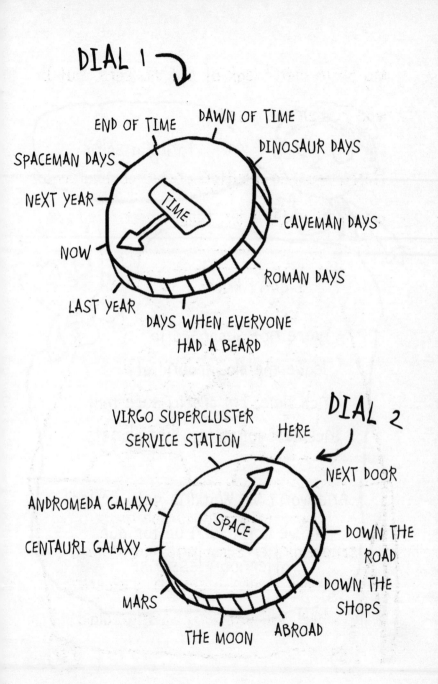

DIAL 1

END OF TIME

DAWN OF TIME

SPACEMAN DAYS

DINOSAUR DAYS

NEXT YEAR

TIME

CAVEMAN DAYS

NOW

ROMAN DAYS

LAST YEAR

DAYS WHEN EVERYONE
HAD A BEARD

VIRGO SUPERCLUSTER
SERVICE STATION

HERE

DIAL 2

ANDROMEDA GALAXY

NEXT DOOR

SPACE

CENTAURI GALAXY

DOWN THE
ROAD

DOWN THE
SHOPS

MARS

THE MOON

ABROAD

Fancy a spin?
I don't know.
We're not supposed to leave the playground at lunch time. I'm pretty sure that includes going to other planets.
And won't Mr Watkins get worried if we don't turn up for our afternoon lessons?

It's fine. We can return to the same time we left. We could be gone for days and return just a few seconds later.

'What could possibly go wrong?' I thought, as I jumped into the bin and clicked on my seatbelt.

Harry twisted the space dial and the bin rumbled violently. For a moment we lurched upwards as if we were in a supersonic lift. Then the bin came to an abrupt stop and the lid opened.

CHAPTER FIVE

The first thing I should say is that space is

AWESOME.

We had a snowball fight on an ice planet in the Black-Eye Galaxy.

I tasted the Fried Aldebaran Chicken, an animal so delicious it's extinct in over 500 solar systems.

We visited a planet in the Andromeda Galaxy where the main form of transport is water slide.

The next thing I should say is that the future is

AWESOME.

We tried on hover shoes.

We watched a film in 5D.

We played a game where the graphics were BETTER than real life.

The other thing I should say is that the past ISN'T VERY AWESOME.

AT ALL.

I should have listened to Harry.

I don't think we should go back to the past. You have to be very careful. Every little thing you do could change the world for ever.

Imagine if you dropped your watch and cavemen found it. They'd invent the bus timetable before the wheel!

Bus Stop

Well take me back to the days BEFORE cavemen then. I'll hardly be able to do any damage there, will I?

Please, please, please, please, PLEASE!

This works on my parents.

Hmm. Go on then. But don't touch ANYTHING.

Harry turned the dial ...

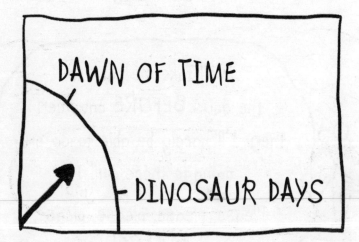

DAWN OF TIME

DINOSAUR DAYS

CHAPTER SIX

We were standing on a soft, yellow beach looking out at a calm, blue sea.

Harry pointed to the lapping waves, where a small, green creature was bobbing about near the shore.

Keep perfectly still. It mustn't see you.

Why? Is it dangerous?

No, it's you. Or it will be. These are the creatures that eventually become humans. I thought you might like to see their first steps.

They don't look much like humans.

They develop into you. Look . . .

As the creature waddled past, Harry held his space communicator above it, and scanned it. A diagram appeared on the screen.

That must have been when the bad thing happened. Although Harry didn't know it, he'd just RUINED THE WORLD.

CHAPTER SEVEN

I knew something was wrong as soon as
we landed.

There was a dinner lady standing at the edge of the playground.

She turned around.

It was worse than I could ever have imagined ...

It wasn't a dinner lady at all.
IT WAS MR WATKINS!!!

It's like talking to a brick wall.

But why was he dressed as a dinner lady?

We rushed around the corner, where some little kids were playing.

They turned around ...

AAAAARRRRGGGHHH!!!

They all looked exactly like Mr Watkins too.

As I looked across the playground, the horrible truth sank in. Everyone looked and sounded exactly like Mr Watkins. Maybe we hadn't returned to Earth at all.

Maybe we'd landed on the PLANET NIGHTMARE.

57

This is all our fault!
What!!???!!
This is what should have happened to that sea creature we saw . . .

Why did we have to turn everyone in the world into boring teachers?

This was the worst thing that could ever have happened.

Why couldn't we have turned everyone in the world into awesome killer robots?

Or cool werewolves?

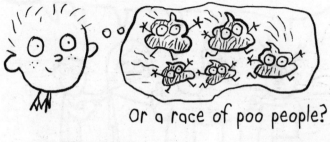

Or a race of poo people?

Even if they'd kept on being sea creatures
it would have been better.

We tried to go back to the bin, but the Mr Watkins creatures swarmed around it.

They unlocked the doors of the gym and wheeled the spacebin inside.

Then they turned to us.

We rushed out of the gates and down the road. The Mr Watkins people chased us, their moustaches twitching.

We ducked into an alley and pushed ourselves against the wall. I held my breath as the creatures approached ...

They ran past.

I sighed with relief.

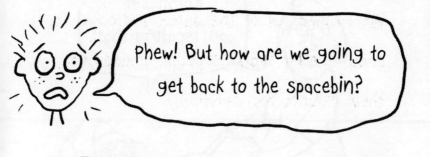

Phew! But how are we going to get back to the spacebin?

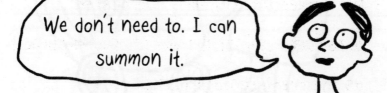

We don't need to. I can summon it.

Harry took out his communicator and was about to press a button on it when two more Mr Watkins creatures appeared.

These ones were so hideous we both froze on the spot ...

The woman grabbed Harry's communicator, threw it into her pram and scurried back to the school.

We ran after her, but this only made the other Mr Watkins creatures spot us.

They turned and pelted towards us, chanting the word 'detention'.

We dashed down the alley, ducking
overhanging washing and leaping
over puddles.

The alley led us to a main road. The street
was deserted, but the horrific influence of
Mr Watkins was still everywhere ...

The creatures were stomping down the alley

behind us, and the chants of 'detention'

were getting louder.

We need to hide somewhere!

I saw a games shop. The lights were off, but the door was slightly open.

QUICK! In there!

CHAPTER EIGHT

We slammed the shop doors shut and crouched on the floor.

I could hear the creatures stomping around outside.

Eventually, they went off down the street, their chants fading away.

I got up and glanced around the shelves. Every game I could see had Mr Watkins on the cover and looked incredibly boring.

DETENTION MASTER

WASHING-UP: THE GAME

CONFISCATION STATION

HOMEWORK DUTY

I saw one that I thought was a driving game, but it turned out to be a traffic jam simulator ... BORING!

We don't have time to look at the games!

That's okay. They're pretty rubbish anyway.

I don't know what to do. They've got my spacebin and my communicator.

I was sort of expecting you to know what to do. You've got more experience of time and space travel than me.

But I've never been anywhere as horrible as this before. Maybe we should surrender and reason with them.

No. We're the only people in this world who don't look and sound exactly like Mr Watkins.

You know what that makes us? Freaks! We'll be prodded by scientists and locked in a zoo, where people with bristly moustaches will stare at us every day.

So what should we do?

I grabbed a marker pen and a stack of paper from behind the counter and tried to come up with a plan.

PLAN ONE: WE TUNNEL INTO THE GYM AND FIND THE SPACEBIN.

But we might tunnel into the detention prison by mistake.

PLAN FOUR: WE SHAVE OUR HEADS AND WEAR FAKE MOUSTACHES. WE LIVE AMONG THE WATKINS CREATURES AND EARN THEIR TRUST UNTIL THEY GIVE US THE KEYS TO THE GYM.

Nothing I thought of seemed right. Soon I gave up and started doodling instead.

I glanced down at my rude drawings. They gave me an idea. This time it seemed like it might work.

I told Harry about my plan.

I don't know. It seems like a risk.

It's our only chance! We've got to try!

CHAPTER NINE

We watched the sun rise over the school from the alleyway. The Mr Watkins creatures started arriving just before nine.

Cars pulled up outside the gates. Hairy mums and dads got out and said goodbye to their identical, hairy children.

I squirmed with disgust as a Mr Watkins woman kissed her Mr Watkins daughter on the cheek, their moustaches brushing.

Soon the playground was full and it was
time for our plan to begin.

Soon all the Mr Watkins creatures were staring at me. I threw a screwed-up piece of paper into the playground.

It bounced off the shiny head of one of the adult Mr Watkins creatures.

Sorry, sir. I was aiming for the bin.

There was silence for a moment as the Mr Watkins clones looked down at the paper. Then they shouted at the top of their voices:

DETENTION!

I lobbed all my other bits of screwed-up paper through the railings. Soon all the Mr Watkins creatures were purple with anger.

The creatures charged out of the gates, growling through their moustaches. I waited for them in the alley, grinning and waving.

When they were almost upon me, I turned and ran.

The Mr Watkins creatures followed, shoving each other out of the way to get to me.

The Mr Watkins creatures gasped as they piled out into the street ...

We'd stayed up all night covering every surface with drawings of Mr Watkins.

We'd painted them on windows, chalked them on paving stones and scrawled them on every piece of paper we could find.

The Mr Watkins creatures looked at us, then at the pictures, gurgling and spluttering with rage.

They stormed out into the street and began to tear down the posters, wipe away the paintings and rub away the chalk with their feet.

It was just as I'd hoped. Like Mr Watkins himself, the creatures were unable to ignore rude pictures.

I ran back down the alley into the school playground, which was now completely abandoned.

The doors to the gym had been forced open.

Harry was in.

CHAPTER TEN

Through the dim light of the high windows, I could see a mountain of catapults, balls and bats. They clattered to the ground as Harry rummaged through them.

This is the confiscation room
for the whole town.

Every time one of the Mr Watkins
creatures invents something interesting
by mistake it's confiscated and brought
here. The spacebin and communicator
must be here somewhere.

I peered out through the door. I could
see a couple of the Mr Watkins creatures
beyond the railings. Surely they couldn't
have removed all the pictures already?

I could hear a distant murmur of 'detention' starting up again.

Hold them off!

I slammed the doors shut and grabbed a dusty cricket bat out of the pile. I jammed it between the door handles. It would hold, but not for long.

Harry was frantically flinging stuff about now. There was still no sign of the spacebin.

I scanned around the dingy room, hoping to see the green plastic of the spacebin in one of the piles.

There was a doorway at the end of the room.

DO NOT ENTER! DANGER OF DETENTION

Look! It must be through there!

CHAPTER ELEVEN

We ran down a stone corridor into a large room with an arched ceiling.

Multicoloured light streamed in through stained-glass windows.

There it was. The spacebin was in the middle of the room, next to a golden desk.

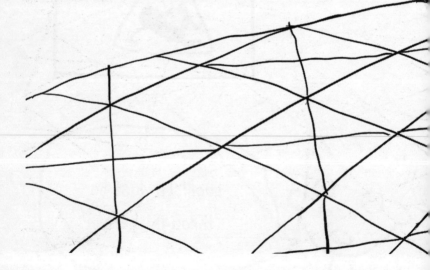

GREAT! Let's jump in!

I can't. I need to find my communicator.

Harry yanked the desk drawer open.
A piercing alarm ran out and one of the
Mr Watkins dinner ladies barged in.

She grabbed Harry by the neck and pinned
him against the wall.

I looked around the room for something to distract the creature. I wouldn't be able to overpower her, but if I could make her angry, she might leave Harry alone and come after me.

I walked into a bright shaft of light beneath one of the windows. A tiny reflection appeared on the wall next to my wrist.

Of course! Watch shine would make her mad!

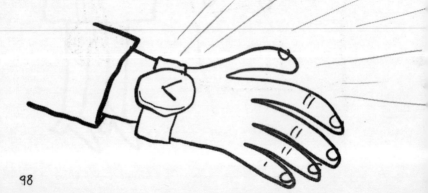

I twisted my wrist around until the reflection
fell on the face of the Mr Watkins creature.

She turned away from Harry and roared.

The Mr Watkins creature leapt at me. She was snorting loudly and a vein on her forehead was pulsing.

There was a crash from outside, followed by stamping feet. The other creatures were in the building.

Harry rooted around in the drawer, flinging rings, bracelets and necklaces aside.

The other Mr Watkins creatures piled into the room chanting, 'DETENTION!'

They were almost upon us when Harry held up the communicator.

GOT IT!

He pressed a button on the front and the spacebin flipped open. I had never imagined I could be so pleased about climbing into a stinky bin.

I barely had time to click my seatbelt on when the spacebin started rumbling and rocketed upwards.

First we have to race back to the dawn of time and stop the moustache hair falling on the sea creature. Then humans can develop as normal.

Now, make sure you don't touch anything except the hair. And DON'T talk to yourself.

I mean don't talk to the past version of yourself that you're about to meet. And don't ask why you can't remember meeting yourself in the past. Your brain really WOULD leak out your ears if I tried to explain that.

CHAPTER TWELVE

We were back on the beach in the distant past. I looked around for our past selves, knowing that I'd just have a few seconds to save the human race when we appeared out of the bin.

Harry scanned the sand with his communicator.

This is it. This is the exact spot we'll appear in.

There was a loud pop.

The spacebin appeared just a few metres down the beach.

Well, I was nearly right.

Identical versions of us jumped out and wandered up to the sea.

Harry (now) Me (now) Me (then) Harry (then)

The sea creature waddled across the sand. The other Harry held his communicator above it.

Quick! Grab the hair!

I sprinted over, trying not to tread in any piles of sea-creature poo that were lying around on the sand.

I could see it. The tiny hair on the end of the communicator was fluttering in the breeze.

It blew up in the air. In just a couple of seconds, it would fall on the sea creature and change humanity forever.

But I wasn't close enough. I was going to have to jump.

As I was flying through the air I wondered what would happen if I caught the hair but squashed the sea creature. Would the whole human race turn out as flat as pancakes?

Or would I wipe us out altogether?

Luckily, I didn't have to find out. I grasped the hair and crashed to the ground just next to the creature.

It looked at me in confusion. So did 'me'. The other me, I mean.

Come to think of it, I was pretty confused too.

Other me

Who are you? Why do you look like me? Why did you grab that hair?

I remembered what Harry had said about not talking to myself, so I stayed quiet. I felt quite rude, but I was only being rude to myself. I'm sure I didn't mind.

I raced back across the beach with the hair clasped in my hand, and jumped into the spacebin.

CHAPTER THIRTEEN

The lid of the spacebin opened, and we climbed out.

We walked around the corner into the playground. A teacher was standing with his back to us. He turned round ...

AAARRGHHH! It was one of the Mr Watkins creatures!

You're going the right way for a detention.

My heart sank. What had gone wrong?
Why hadn't we wiped them out?

A little further on, some little kids were
playing.

They turned around ...

Phew! They were normal.

I looked around the playground.

None of the pupils had shiny bald heads or thick moustaches.

It wasn't a Mr Watkins clone I'd seen.

It was the actual Mr Watkins.

The ONLY Mr Watkins.

I looked back at Mr Watkins and smiled. It was the first time I'd ever been pleased to see him.

What's so amusing, Colin? Perhaps you'd like to share it?

I'm just pleased that everyone isn't like you. They're normal!

WHAT?!?!

Er . . . what Colin means is that you're an abnormally brilliant teacher and there's no one else like you. That's why he's so happy.
Well in that case I'll let it pass. But don't let me catch you near those bins again.

It was only when I sat down for my afternoon lesson that I realized how exhausted I was.

Although we'd only been missing for a few seconds, our adventure had lasted hours. And I'd gone a whole night without sleeping.

My chances of staying awake were zero.

Luckily, Mr Watkins closed the blinds and put a DVD on, so I flopped forward and drifted off to sleep ...

CHAPTER FOURTEEN

The next few days were blissfully normal.
I was still bored senseless by Mr Watkins,
but I was so relieved there was only one
of him, I didn't really mind.

I was just thinking about our spacebin
adventure when the lights on Harry's
communicator flashed.

I ran after Harry and caught up with him
as he was walking out into the playground.

You're off again, aren't
you? Let me come!

I can't. It's too
dangerous.

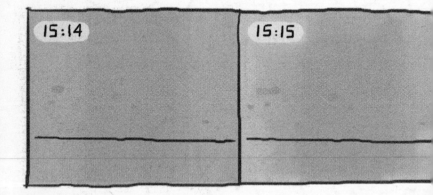

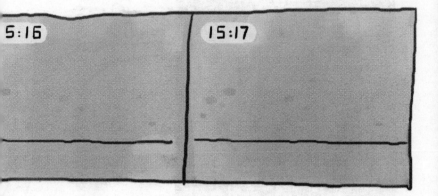